Get down to the bookstore
for the first Bad Dog books!
Bad Dog and That Hollywood Hoohah
Bad Dog and Those Crazy Martians

And look out for the next fur-raising adventure:
Bad Dog Goes Barktastic!

BAD DOG

AND THE CURSE OF THE PRESIDENT'S KNEE

MARTIN CHATTERTON

SCHOLASTIC INC.

New York   Toronto   London   Auckland   Sydney
Mexico City   New Delhi   Hong Kong   Buenos Aires

No part of this work may be reproduced, stored in a retrieval
system, or transmitted in any form or by any means, electronic,
mechanical, photocopying, recording, or otherwise, without
written permission of the publisher. For information regarding
permission, write to Scholastic Ltd., Commonwealth House,
1–19 New Oxford Street, London WC1A 1NU, United Kingdom.

ISBN 0-439-66160-9

Text and illustrations copyright © 2004 by Martin Chatterton

All rights reserved. Published by Scholastic Inc., 557 Broadway,
New York, NY 10012, by arrangement with Scholastic Ltd.

SCHOLASTIC, APPLE PAPERBACKS, and associated logos are
trademarks and/or registered trademarks of Scholastic Inc.

12 11 10 9 8 7 6 5 4 3 2 1   5 6 7 8 9 10 / 0

Printed in the U.S.A.   40
First Scholastic printing, May 2005

CHAPTER 1

MY NAME IS BAD DOG

"My name is Bad Dog," I said, getting to my feet. "And I'm a cataholic."

There was a pretty good ripple of warm applause from the circle of dogs watching me. I wiped a tear from my eye. A speck of dust had blown in it, honest.

I was at my very first Cataholics Anonymous meeting. You know that Alcoholics Anonymous is for people who want to stop drinking alcohol, right? And Gamblers Anonymous is for people who want to stop gambling? Well, Cataholics Anonymous is for dogs who want to stop chasing cats. And boy, do I need to stop doing that.

I'm locked up here in the City Dog Pound. My crime? I'm a dog.

Worse, I'm a dog on Z-Block, which is the place where all the problem dogs end up. If we go through that stinking green door at the end of the corridor, we don't come back. Ever. For those of you busy picking your nose or scratching your behind, that means we get *killed*.

Oh, do I have your attention now?

And when I tell you that I've been plucked from this pooch pit not once but *twice*, only to find myself bounced right back in here all because of *cats*, you'll get some clue as to why I figured that trying CA wasn't a bad idea.

See, I *hate* cats. I hate their nasty little feline ways: the way they lick their paws, the way they hiss, their disgusting yowling, the way they don't sleep at night like ordinary guys.

And what are cats actually *for*? I mean, dogs are always dashing around rescuing people trapped in mines, or pulling kids out of icy lakes, or running back into town to tell the sheriff that little Ricky's been kidnapped by Black Jack McCallaghan and is tied to the railroad track with the 3:10 to Yuma

comin' round the bend. Us dogs *work*. We round up sheep, sniff out explosives, dig up skiers buried in avalanches, guide blind people across city streets, chase down crooks, fetch the newspaper, get blasted into outer space, pull sleds in Alaska . . . all kinds of useful stuff.

What do cats do? Sit on fences, wail like babies all night, and sleep on the sofa. I rest my case.

My favorite show is *Tom & Jerry* 'cause that cat gets it, right in the face, every freakin' time, right?

"You *love* cats!" said a voice, snapping me out of my happy Exploding Cat daydream. It was Reverend Bentley Sweetlord the Fourth, my "cat counselor." Every pound has someone like Bentley. He'd arrived four years ago with a real tough-guy street rep. A huge beast of a dog, weighing in at something around the size of a hippo, he'd been leader of the fearsome East Side Reservoir Dogs. The dog catchers had been after Bentley for years, and one day they finally got him.

Being inside didn't cramp his style too much. He was still the dog nobody messed with. If you needed anything on the inside and had something to trade, Bentley was the dog who would get it for you. At a price. He'd been inside so long he knew all the dodges, all the scams. He was top dog down in the yard. And then, about a year back, something happened.

After a particularly vile plate of chow, Bentley Sweetlord the Fourth had come down with a fever. In the grip of this fever he had a vision that changed his life completely. The vision came to him in the shape of a purple fish wearing a skirt (Hey, it's Bentley's vision, OK?), and told him to give up his old ways and devote the rest of his life to helping dogs and cats live together in peace and harmony. When he woke up he told everyone to call him Reverend.

Reverend Bentley was holding up a small pink stuffed toy cat. "Repeat after me, Bad Dog: 'I *love* cats!'"

I goggled. What? Say *what*? Like, *no* feline way. I became aware of the audience looking at me expectantly. They all had their best puppy-dog faces on.

"Come on, man," whispered Reverend Bentley. He turned back to the audience and raised his voice. "Wake up and smell the coffee. Learn to love The Cat. Be its friend. Give yourself over to The Power of LUUURVE!"

"Amen, brother!" barked a big crossbred lurcher from the back.

"You know it!" shouted a tiny, three-legged Jack Russell, his eyes closed and face lifted to the ceiling. A murmur of "Right on!" and "Yeah!" spread through the crowd. I could feel they wanted me to make the step.

"I-I-I . . ." I stuttered.

"That's it, Brother Bad Dog!" said Reverend Bentley Sweetlord the Fourth. "Let it out. Let it all out! Let the luurve show through, bright and shining, clean and pure!"

"I . . . lo . . ." I coughed, the words sticking in my throat.

Bentley lifted the fluffy little toy cat nearer to me. "Cats are good," said the Reverend. "Feel the force, my brother!"

"I lo-lo-love . . ." I said, my face inches from the cat.

The audience inched forward expectantly. Bentley wiggled the toy cat in front of me, and suddenly I felt something shift deep in my stomach. Barging Bentley to the floor, I seized the cat doll in my teeth and, in a blur of fury and stuffing, I ripped that little sucker into a thousand pieces.

"I LOVE . . . *MESSING UP CATS!*" I bellowed into the shocked silence, a crazed expression of blood-lust etched into my face.

It looked like Reverend Bentley and Cataholics Anonymous had their work cut out.

I will say this: In the days that followed, they didn't give up on me. Reverend Bentley had me in Cat Aversion Therapy. He would flash a picture of a happy, smiling cat in front of me and give me a doggy treat. (Don't ask me where he got his supply; you don't ask questions like that in the slammer. Not if you want to keep all your teeth, anyway.) Then he would show me a picture of a dog chasing a cat. If I smiled, or barked approvingly, he'd whack me over the skull with his "medicine" — a length of lumber he kept handy for just that purpose.

"Take your medicine," he'd say. "Learn to love the cat."

Naturally, I learned to smile at the happy cats and frown when I saw a chased one. "Ooh, tut tut," I'd say, pursing my lips and inwardly thinking about sinking my fangs into the repulsive thing. He spent days devising tests for me. He'd wait till I was asleep in my cell, then slowly drag a dummy cat past me on a piece of string, inches from my nose, to see if I'd react. A couple of times Bentley got dragged fifteen yards before I realized he was still holding the line.

In the exercise yard, he put on cat makeup (a truly hideous sight, see below) and insisted on being my "cat-buddy" for the day.

If we hadn't been in a maximum security dog pound where cats are obviously fairly scarce, he'd have had me cuddling up to some real live kitties in a flash.

But you know the crazy thing about the Rev's loony stunts? Little by little they began to work. He was grinding me down. I began to lose interest in chasing cats. Really — me! Bad Dog, the scourge of the feline world! This may have had something to do with the fine collection of fleshy bumps I was collecting on my noggin from Bentley's "medicine." Or could it be that I was actually starting to see things from a cat point of view?

I glanced at the Cataholics Anonymous pamphlet I'd been instructed to carry with me.

"You must put aside instinct," it said, "and become a New Dog." I took a deep breath and trotted over to Bentley.

"Meow," I said.

CHAPTER 2

OH, SAY CAN YOU SEE?

I found that my new love of cats made me a much more relaxed pooch. I smiled all the time, held doors open for aged doggies, and became generally regarded by one and all as a Pretty Good Egg.

This was my third stint behind bars in Z-Block and I didn't hold out much hope of lightning striking three times in one place. But one damp morning in October, with my cell creeping uncomfortably close to the Green Door, I was busy doing some advanced yoga techniques (which, to the untrained eye, could have looked exactly like I was fast asleep) when I heard a commotion in the corridor. There was a crackle of electrostatic and the sound of clipped foot-steps. A very large guy trotted past me, gave me a blank stare, and stationed himself against the Green Door. He wore a gray suit with a black tie. His right hand rested on something just inside his jacket. His left shielded a small microphone which he whispered into. "Daffy Duck to Yosemite Sam. Daffy Duck to Yosemite Sam. Objective one achieved. Copy."

I couldn't hear the reply, but the guy nodded as if whoever had spoken was standing just in front of him. "Affirmative, Operation Scooby-Doo initiated," said the guy. "Over."

This looked . . . interesting.

I looked down the line of dirty cells and saw two more big guys in suits and shades walking along. They were looking around and down and up and were talking into microphones. Behind them was a smartly dressed fella grinning like a maniac. A TV crew was following him. Behind the TV crew were two more big suit/shades-type guys and a whole batch of hangers-on, reporter-types, and cameramen flashing photos. Bringing up the rear was Fester, our block commandant, who had combed his hair for some reason.

The grinning guy looked familiar. I was sure I had seen him somewhere, but couldn't quite put my paw on where. I looked down at the floor of my cell. There were some old newspapers spread on the floor mopping up a little "accident" I'd had earlier. Hey, it wasn't my fault they only let us out of the cells twice a day.

There, on the front page of the newspaper, was the grinning guy under a big headline:

THE POST

President Buckenberger Agrees Budget Cuts

The President today agreed a wide range of national budget measures aimed at reducing the federal deficit to pre-nineties levels.
He okayed several key senate initiatives to levy higher residuals from the budget. All measures are to be in place before the start of the new fiscal year, a Treasury spokesman said when asked.

That grinning guy in the corridor was the freakin' Prez! Our Fearless Leader! The Most Important Big Cheese Guy In The Whole World!!! Here! Right smack dab in front of me!!!!!

I decided to play things very cool, and immediately began shouting, "Hey, Prez! Hey, Prez! Look at me! Look at me!" over and over again, while bouncing around the cell.

President Buckenberger came to a stop in front of my cell, turned his back to me, and began to give a speech to the media people. He ignored the racket I was making.

"People of America," he said solemnly, as though everyone in America had suddenly crowded into Z-Block. "It's nice to be here in Las Vegas."

There was a small cough from behind the Prez and a scary-looking woman whispered something in his ear.

"It's nice to be here in Los Angeles," continued the Prez, unruffled. "As some of you will be aware, my dog, Rupert, recently passed away in a tragic accident involving a hedge trimmer and a garden hose. Myself and Mrs. President have been very upset about our loss." He paused and dabbed at his eye with the corner of a hankie. "This is the reason I'm here today at this wonderful, caring institution: to choose another dog for the White House."

I wondered why the Prez had stopped in front of my cell. Suddenly, the penny dropped — right next to me was King, a large, not-quite-German shepherd, who had got on the wrong side of everyone with his big-headed attitude. Fester had been grooming King all day, and now I knew why. The Prez was here to take King to the White House! No wonder King'd been grinning like a fool. This was more than me and my big head could stand. No beefed-up Bavarian was going to get that gig without a fight from yours truly.

As I was in full view of the cameras, I began to turn on the charm.

I chased my tail.

I played dead.

I did card tricks.

I acted out some of my favorite movie scenes.

The media pack began to nudge one another and look at me. More cameras began to swivel my way and the Prez began to notice. As he turned around, I stood and saluted him and barked out a few bars of "The Star-Spangled Banner."

He gave me a slightly confused smile and then turned back to the cameras.

"Like America, the dog I choose will be strong! Determined! Friendly! And like America, he will be made up of many, er, sorts of breeds, erm, dog, er . . . not that Americans are like dogs, no sir!

But we are many proud very good things, and independent! Yes." The Prez stuttered to a halt, perhaps trying to make sense of what he'd just said. The cameras kept rolling. It didn't seem to matter to the media that the president was talking gibberish. They were obviously used to it. Just then the tall, scary-looking woman leaned forward and there was a whispered exchange that, thanks to my super-doggy sense of hearing and incredible nosiness, I managed to overhear.

"Small change of plan, sir," she hissed. "We're going with this one." She jerked a thumb in my direction.

"What!" said the Prez. "What happened to King? I kinda like German shepherds."

"King's history, sir. The cameras love this one for some reason," said the woman, looking at me like I was something she'd just stepped in. "We're getting some numbers in and they are *huge*. I say go with the mutt. His name's Bad Dog . . . just call him BD."

King, of course, had picked all this up, too, and was kicking up so much noise that one of the Secret Service guys had to gently tap him on the noggin with the butt of his gun to remind him that the president was speaking.

President Buckenberger gave me a puzzled look before pasting his grin back on and turning back to the cameras. "And so, fellow Americans, I'd like to introduce the newest White House staff member, BD Buckenberger!"

He turned and gestured to me. Fester snapped the lock open and dozens of cameras clicked and flashed. I'd done it again! I was free.

CHAPTER 3

ELVIS HAS LEFT THE BUILDING

"Er," I said. And that was as far as I got before a couple of suits grabbed me, clipped a leash on, and handed me over to the Prez.

In a whirl of excitement I was bundled out of the City Pound in the president's limo. Daffy Duck was sitting across from me, next to his partner, Yosemite Sam. They weren't smiling. We raced through the city in a four-car motorcade, six motorcycle escorts in front and back, sirens wailing.

We went straight through red lights, stopping for no one. In a few minutes we were on board the president's plane and on our way to Washington, D.C..

President Buckenberger turned out to be a pretty good guy. He may have spoken English like it was his second language, but he sure liked dogs.

"Hey fella!" said the Prez. "Don't be scared of the plane." He tickled the top of my head. I didn't have the heart to tell him that, far from being scared, I was having the time of my life.

The Prez asked for a stick. Instantly, a fabbo stick was produced, a proper wooden one with nice chewy bits of twig on it. I figured that when you were President of the United States, if you asked for something, you got it. He threw it down the aisle.

"Go on, fella! Fetch!"

Now normally I don't fetch for anyone, but as this *was* the Prez and he was being real nice, I decided to humor him. Besides, how many times do you get a chance to play "fetch" at 35,000 feet?

Some of the staff were gathered around a TV set watching the news. I squeezed through for a look, and there I was up on the screen! Behind the TV reporter I could see a commotion as King tried to eat his way out of Z-Block.

"What I don't understand," the Prez was saying to the scary-looking lady, "is why we need two dogs at the White House? Don't get me wrong, I'm glad to have him along." He bent and tickled my head. "But why two?"

The scary lady sighed as if she had been over all this stuff before. "Because two dogs make you look generous," she said. "Sir."

"Yes, yes, I suppose you're right," said the Prez.

"I'm always right," she muttered in a voice too low to have been heard by anyone but me.

"It's looking good, Mr. President," said a chubby guy sitting hunched forward over a monitor. "The folks down there like having a new dog in the White House."

"Well, so do I, Clay." President Buckenberger smiled. "So do I."

I was really starting to like this guy. But what was all that about two dogs?

After a while President Buckenberger sat down at a big desk and began to sign important-looking papers. I started to have a look around. One of the advantages of being a dog is that you can walk around being nosy, and no one even notices you.

Well, almost no one.

As I padded around the cushioned luxury of Air Force One, I became aware of a pair of eyes following me. Not wanting to rock the boat so early, I lay down and pretended to go to sleep. Then I opened one eye a sliver and scoped the area. The eyes that had been fixed on me belonged to the tall, severe-looking woman who had been whispering in the Prez's ear at the pound. Now she was sitting just behind President Buckenberger, passing him papers.

"Thank you, Ms. Masters," he said.

"Sir," she murmured, her eyes flicking sideways, watching what I was doing.

She was the White House Chief of Staff, a fact I'd picked up because she mentioned it about ten times a minute. I'd noticed that she had everyone jumping through hoops around here.

Ms. Masters had a thick head of jet-black hair styled in a rigid helmet around her narrow face. Dark eyes. Thin nose. A wide mouth with sharp little teeth. I began to feel uneasy.

And then, because I'm a dog, I forgot all about her and fell fast asleep.

I woke up as we touched down in Washington. The Prez stepped off the plane with me at his heels and the cameras flashed again. Into the motorcade. Sirens. Motorcycle cops. Red lights. We sped through the city and right into the White House itself.

Bad Dog had arrived! This was fantastic. Limos, fame, good food, plenty of sleep, and soft fluffy blankets lay ahead of me like an endless Christmas.

As we were driving in, another car was driving out, a Secret Service bod behind the wheel looking very unhappy.

I noticed a large suitcase on the back seat of his car as it slid past. He didn't wave to Daffy Duck or Yosemite Sam, who looked at him blankly.

I scampered out of the limo and ran towards the White House, where Mrs. President stood waiting for her husband (and new dog) to arrive. Nothing could spoil my mood. I was on Cloud Nine. Happy as could be. You get the picture. And just as I reached the steps, feeling about as good as a dog can get without finding a fresh brontosaurus bone, I saw it sitting in the doorway.

A cat. In *my* White House.

CHAPTER 4

THAT PRICKLY FEELING

No, I didn't chase that cat.

Bentley would've been proud of me. I just repeated under my breath, "My name is Bad Dog. I am a cataholic."

And it did the trick. I walked up the steps and right up to the cat without feeling any desire to bark loudly and give chase. Well, hardly any.

"How do you do?" I said. "My name is Bad Dog."

The cat looked at me from hooded eyes.

"Vernon Sangster, White House Chief of Cats. And I'm very well, thanks," he said, offering a paw. "So you're number seven, eh? I hope you know how to take care of yourself."

He gave me a sly look. *Was that a warning?* I thought. And what was that about "number seven"?

I was thinking about grabbing Vernon and working off some energy upside his head when I heard Bentley's voice echoing from my memory banks, and I contented myself with sitting down and sniffing my rear.

Just then I heard the familiar sound of dog paws clacking across the floor. I turned and saw a medium-sized dog walking slowly towards us. I held out a friendly paw. The new dog just looked at it.

"Oh," said Vernon. "Let me introduce

you." He smiled slyly. "Bad Dog, meet Rover. Rover, Bad Dog." I turned, paw raised to say, "Hi."

The dog said nothing. He looked me up and down and turned to Vernon.

"I don't think this one will last long, Sangster," he said in an unpleasant growl. "Doesn't look like he has much pedigree."

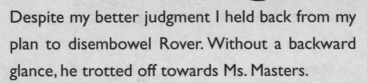

I was about to show Rover my street-fightin' pedigree when Vernon caught my eye. He shook his head and held up a paw. Despite my better judgment I held back from my plan to disembowel Rover. Without a backward glance, he trotted off towards Ms. Masters.

"You need to watch that one," said Vernon. "I know Rover's one of your lot, but you need to take a long hard look at him. He's in tight with Masters, and she's one lady you don't want to upset."

I was about to reply when Mrs. President rushed over, gathered Vernon Sangster up in her arms, and waved to the Prez. "Darling!" Mrs. Prez shrieked in a high-pitched screech, almost deafening me. The woman had a voice that could be used as a weapon of mass destruction. She clattered down the steps and gave President Buckenberger a bone-crunching hug. They waved to the cameras one last time and disappeared past me into the White House. I trotted in behind them and found myself in a surprisingly small hallway.

As soon as the Buckenbergers set foot inside the White House, the grins fell from their faces and they leaped apart as though each thought the other was radioactive. President Buckenberger actually seemed to shrink slightly, while Mrs. Buckenberger positively crackled with fury.

"And what, precisely, is *that* all about?" said Mrs. Prez, pointing a bony finger in my direction.

"Well, er, it's like this, honey . . ." stuttered the Prez.

"Central Office thought that replacing Rupert quickly would play well with the voters, Mrs. Buckenberger," said Ms. Masters in a steely tone. "And we can't ignore the voters, now can we?"

She smiled brightly at Mrs. President and, turning on her pointed black heels, clipped off down the marble hall with Rover following close behind. That dog really was a creep. A strange little man I hadn't seen before trotted along at Ms. Masters' side. He looked a bit like a successful experiment to combine a human with a lizard. The three of them stopped at a well-guarded door and, flashing a security pass at the marine on duty, slipped out of sight.

Back in the hallway, Mrs. President looked as if she was about to snarl something after Ms. Masters, then thought better of it and contented herself with having a good sulk.

"Ye-es, well, just make sure you keep that thing away from Vernon," she hissed at her husband and stomped away in the opposite direction, the cat clutched high in the air, as if I might suddenly leap on it and rip its head off. Maybe she had a point, after all.

Vernon wiggled his paw at me over her shoulder and winked as they disappeared from view.

"Er, righto then," said the Prez. "I have Some Very Important Papers to go over. I shall be in the Green Room. I am not to be disturbed." I don't know who he was talking to, because there was only me left. And, of course, the Secret Service guys.

He walked briskly away down the corridor followed by three of them. They were still talking into their little microphones to each other and looking around warily, as if expecting a bunch of ninjas to drop down from the White House ceiling at any minute. Then one of the Secret Service dudes, the one code-named Daffy Duck, slowed down and began walking jerkily. One of the others noticed this and walked back. He glanced around to check that no one was looking, reached around to the back of Daffy's head, and pressed a thumb into a point on his neck. Instantly Daffy perked up, and the two of them rejoined the Prez. The whole thing had taken only a couple of seconds.

No one took any notice of me.

"Hmm," I said, or at least I would have, except that no one says "hmm" really. I just thought that there were one or two things that needed investigation.

I decided to take a look around.

The first thing you notice about being in the White House is that it's a busy place. Lots and lots of people work there. There were Secret Service people everywhere, official-looking bods in fancy clothes carrying papers, people repairing phones, installing drinking fountains. And there were soldiers all over the place.

After some time, I came to a strange, gloomy corridor somewhere deep in the bowels of the White House.

I picked up an odd sound on the hairy antenna. My ears, thicko. The sound was coming from behind a door with a sign on it which read: ABSOLUTELY NO ADMITTANCE. TOP SECRET. AUTHORIZED PERSONNEL ONLY. BY ORDER OF THE FEDERAL GOVERNMENT. Naturally, I nosed it open and stepped in.

Instead of the InterContinental Ballistic Missile Bunker I had expected to see, I found myself in a pleasant lounge, full of comfy chairs and with a big TV set, just like in a regular house. Inside the room President Buckenberger was practicing his putting — the clacking sound I'd heard was golf balls hitting a metal cup he'd placed on the carpet. The TV was on with the sound turned down.

"Oh, hi, fella," said the Prez absentmindedly, looking up briefly from his practice.

"Right back at ya, Prez," I said.

I noticed a silver-framed picture standing on a little knickknack table. It was a picture of a good-looking hound. Not, obviously, as good-looking as me, but still pretty darn handsome.

"Rupert," said the Prez. "He was my favorite, even though he was only here a couple of weeks."

A couple of weeks? I didn't like the sound of that.

I looked at the Prez standing there with his putter talking about the dogs, and a little prickle of . . . something, I don't know what, ran along the back of my neck. I got the feeling I was on the edge of understanding A Very Important Thing. Then a picture of a juicy bone flashed into my mind and the feeling passed.

There were more silver-framed photos dotted around the room. I figured that Rupert must have been very popular with the Buckenbergers, but as I took a closer look, I saw that they were all of different dogs. There must have been six at least: two chihuahuas, a poodle, a Weimaraner, a German shepherd . . . the place was like a Who's Who of dogs. There was one photo of Rover looking like a complete doofus in a plaid waistcoat.

As I looked at each photo the Prez would murmur a name, as if remembering each of the mutts.

"Spotty . . .

Blackie . . .

Toffee . . ."

and so on.

His eyes misted over and he looked out of the window across the lawn. I followed his gaze.

The Prez was looking over toward a heap of stones sitting under a big willow tree. I had the feeling that I should trot over and have a close look at those stones. So that's what I did. I pushed open the French windows and set off across the lawn. It was dark now, with a fat moon casting a blue light across the grass, which was wet underpaw.

As I drew near to the tree, I thought I saw a movement to one side of me and I jerked my head around.

Nothing.

I shivered. This place was giving me the heebie-jeebies. There was something in the dark rustle of the trees and bushes which set my nerves jangling. I could almost hear the spooky music starting up, and I felt like I'd strayed into one of those movies where everyone gets bumped off one by one.

"Get a grip," I muttered to myself. "You're the dog that went to Mars, remember?"

I walked into the shadow of the willow as a cloud passed over the moon, plunging me into total darkness. I could just about make out the stones up ahead in the gloom.

As the cloud drew back, something furry moved silently right in front of me and I leaped three feet into the air.

"Mommy!" I yelped, dropping to the ground and doing my best to hide behind a blade of grass. When that failed I settled for putting my paws over my eyes. After a moment, I risked a peek.

Vernon Sangster was sitting on top of one of the stones, his green eyes watching me.

"Good evening," he said, pleasantly enough. I began to feel more than a tad embarrassed about my naked spinelessness. In front of a cat.

"Er, good evening," I said, coughing. "Did you catch all that 'Mommy' stuff back there?"

"'Fraid so," said Vernon.

"Well, I'd appreciate it if you could, erm, just forget all about it and not mention it to anyone. Particularly any other dogs," I said.

"Forgotten already, old boy," said Vernon. "Besides," he continued, "you've every right to be scared. Take a look." He pointed down at the stones and, for the first time, I saw what they were. Gravestones. The one that Vernon was perched on had RUPERT — RIP engraved on its marble face.

I looked quickly at the others. "Spotty . . . Toffee . . . Blackie . . . Judge . . . Samson."

I felt faint. This was the White House dog grave-yard. I started to babble questions at Vernon but he held up a paw.

"Take a look at the dates," he said in a quiet voice.

I peered closer. All these dogs had bitten the dust within the last three months. It seemed that, on average, a dog could expect to last roughly three weeks at the White House.

"Sheesh," I said. "What happened?"

Vernon sat up and looked at me. "You're the seventh pooch here since May."

"Yes," I said. "But what *happened*? I mean, *how* did they bite the dust? They get sick, or what?"

RUPERT
RIP

"Well, let me see." Vernon put his head to one side. "Samson — he fell out of the presidential helicopter straight into the Potomac."

"Drowned?"

"Poisoned," said Vernon. "Pollution. Toffee copped it when he ate a bad bowl of doggy chow. Judge hit his head on a low table. Blackie tripped and accidentally fell into the presidential washing machine. Spotty chased a cat into the street and got run over by a dump truck. Him, I don't lose much sleep over. Rupert you already know about. And, of course, there's Rover. I don't know how he's managed to stay alive, but he's still here."

He looked at me. "Which is where you come in." He pointed at a dark patch off in the shadows. I trotted over very cautiously to have a look. It was a hole in the ground, freshly dug. The hair on my back stood to attention: The hole was just about my size.

I looked at Vernon. "Is that what I think it is?" My voice had gone very small.

He nodded. "Unless you want to end up sleeping under a stone like this bunch, I suggest you get busy and find out what's happening around here," he said.

"But why are you telling me all this?" I said. "You, well, you're a cat."

"My name is Vernon Sangster," said Vernon. "And I'm a dogaholic."

CHAPTER 5

THE BUTT THAT HAD NO SMELL

Vernon led me back into the White House through a loose metal grate behind some bushes. We squeezed through and I found myself in the boiler room. A huge furnace was roaring away in one corner.

Vernon walked over to a pile of comfortable blankets and settled down to tell me the story.

He hadn't always been in the White House, but he had been with the Buckenbergers for as long as he could remember. Mrs. President, despite having a voice that could strip paint, liked cats just fine, and Vernon enjoyed a life of luxury. Everything in the garden was lovely.

"That lasted until about three months ago," said Vernon. His voice dropped lower. "When the dogs started dying."

The furnace cast flickering red shadows across the room and I shivered, even though it was hotter than a wrestler's underpants in there.

"At first I thought it was just one of those strange coincidences. But by the time Blackie bit the dust I was getting real suspicious. I mean, how does a full-grown dog trip and fall into a top-loading washing machine, *and* manage to switch it on at the same time? It was horrible. He came out of there half-size."

I goggled.

"And here's another thing: They're disappearing faster. The first was three months ago. Then a four week gap, then three weeks, and so on. The life expectancy for a White House dog is now down to about five days."

He took a peek at me as I had a little think about that nugget of information.

"Someone's killing dogs around here and I don't want to wait for them to start on the cat population," said Vernon as he shifted on his haunches. "We've got to find out what's going on. We've got to work together."

Now, I was pretty pleased with my progress as a New Dog, but even so, I choked a little on the idea of actually *helping* a cat.

"I know it's a little weird at first, but think about it," said Vernon. "Just don't take too long."

I was feeling twitchier than a small dog in a large flea circus. Vernon explained that he had come to a similar arrangement with Rupert, and they had been investigating a hot lead when Rupert got snuffed.

"I think we must have been getting close," said Vernon. "And if you don't want to join the rest of them, you could do worse than hitch up with me. There's not a lot about this place I don't know. Sleep on it. I'll contact you tomorrow . . . if you're still here."

He sprang onto a ledge below the grate and slipped out in that silent way that cats have. I decided to find somewhere to plop down for the night. Somewhere safe. I left the boiler room and made my way to the first floor.

The White House was quiet now, with just the odd marine standing guard and the occasional flunky scurrying softly along the carpeted corridors.

My nerves were jangling after Vernon's story and I kept jumping at shadows and whispers. I knew that the White House staff had prepared a real comfy-looking bed for me near the kitchen, but there was no way I was going to sleep where anyone could find me. Not after seeing that fresh grave.

I tried a few doors. Mostly they were empty offices with little computer lights winking in the dark. A few were bedrooms. In one of them I saw something that I immediately filed in a drawer inside my head labeled VERY WEIRD STUFF.

It was an ordinary-looking bedroom. On the bed, fully clothed and wearing shades, were three of the Secret Service guys lying in a neat row, arms by their sides, completely silent. From where I stood I couldn't see any breathing. It was like they had been unplugged for the night.

I thought about investigating further and then decided there was a very good reason not to, namely that I am A Big Chicken, so I closed the door gently and moved off down the corridor. Not far along, I came across a small dark closet in which there was a jumble of bags and boxes. I found a nice big bag and hunkered down for the night. I thought I'd be tossing and turning but I fell asleep instantly.

I woke to find myself bobbing about in the dark. I could hear voices. There was something familiar about them.

"That's a major affirmative, Deputy Dawg. Out."

There was a crackle of static and the voice spoke again. "Huckleberry Hound to Daffy Duck, come in please." Crackle. "Deputy Dawg reports they are in position A. Huckleberry Hound and Pepé Le Pew confirming. Out." There was another crackle.

I fumbled around and found a zipper. I opened it a few inches, peered out, and discovered that I'd gone to sleep in a golf bag. The voices belonged

to two Secret Service guys in a cart behind
the one I seemed to be in, who jumped a mile in
the air when they saw me. They looked around as
if I had just beamed in from an alien spaceship
orbiting the earth. Finding no spaceship, they settled for scowling at me. The golf bag I was sitting
in belonged to the Prez, who was sitting up front
alongside a creepy little guy.

I gave the Prez a friendly woof.

"What's that dog doing here?" he asked the man with him on the cart. The man had hooded eyes with scaly-looking lids, and he looked as if he'd be clammy to the touch. I recognized him — it was the guy I'd seen scuttling along the corridor with Ms. Masters when we'd first arrived at the White House.

"This is your new dog, Mr. President," he said, fixing the Prez with a glare and pressing his fingers into his arm.

"Oh. Yes. Of course, Dr. Okter," said the Prez, looking at me. I wriggled out of the bag and bounced up to him, expect-ing a little pat on the head.

Humans like doing that for some reason, so it's sometimes best to humor them. But the Prez didn't ruffle the fur on my head, or even look at me. Funny, I could have sworn he was a doggy person last night.

He turned and started talking to Lizard Boy (who I now knew was called Okter), and I took the opportunity to sniff around. There was a noise coming from the president's leg; a sort of high-pitched pinging noise, the kind that submarines make in the movies. It was so high-pitched that I was certain only dogs could pick it up. Maybe it was a sort of pacemaker. *Yeah right, genius,* I said to myself. *Who has a heart pacemaker in their leg?*

I crept closer to the Prez and sniffed his butt.

What I smelt was so horrifying that I almost began barking like a maniac there and then. But something stopped me and I held my peace. What had spooked me was this: *The president's butt had no smell.*

Now, I don't mean his butt smelled nice, that he kept it fresh as a rose garden or anything like that. I mean it had *no* smell. It smelled of nothing except the cloth of his pants.

I've sniffed a lot of butts in my time. It's something dogs like to do — don't ask me why, we just do. And one thing I can tell you straight off the bat is that *all* humans have smelly butts. Some are smellier than others, mind you. But they are *all* smelly.

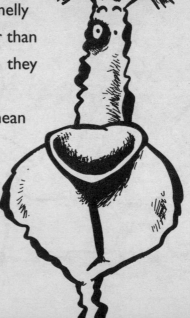

Which could only mean one thing . . . President Buckenberger wasn't human.

CHAPTER 6

DOUBLE BOGEY ON THE TRICKY SIXTH

Well, what could I do? Total panic set in, which I cleverly disguised by acting stupid. I was stranded with a fake president and a guy who looked like he'd be more at home lying on a rock and catching passing flies with his tongue.

I played dumb and decided to wait until I could get together with Vernon before I made any rash moves. Vernon's offer of teaming up to get to the bottom of all this was getting more attractive every minute. There were plenty of important questions I wanted answers to. Like, where was the real Prez? What was this fake president for? What's for dinner?

The fake president and Lizard Boy played golf. I sat in the golf cart and did my best to appear invisible.

I don't know if you've ever watched golf being played. For me it's proof that humans are the dumbest animals on the planet. Okter seemed very interested in Fake President's game, making little notes whenever he hit a shot.

I had time to notice plenty of workmen around the course. They were busy putting up little seating areas, and generally sprucing the place up. I

spotted several banners that read GLISTENING PINES WELCOMES THE 12TH ANNUAL WHITE HOUSE INTERNATIONAL GOLF CHALLENGE! It was due to start in a few days.

From time to time, my super-doggy hearing was picking up a few scraps of conversation.

"It's a long left to right dog leg over water playing from the back tee with a lot of cross fade drop," said Okter.

Fake President seemed to know what all that meant because he replied with another mouthful of gobbledegook. "That last albatross really prettied up the first five out. Let's see if I can hit from a wide stance and let the arc in tight to hit flat and follow low with a real daisy-cutter."

Okter nodded at him approvingly. They were obviously talking in code.

Fake Prez teed off and knocked his little white ball into one of the big sand pits the golfers liked to play in. It was huge, about half the size of the Sahara desert maybe. A bank of grass hid one side from view, with a lake flanked by trees hiding the other.

The fake Prez disappeared from view in search of his ball. I was surprised he didn't take a camel. Okter stayed on the cart, punching information into a little handheld computer and muttering things about "adjustment factors," "circuit damage limitation," and stuff like that. I could see the top of Fake Prez's golf club swinging down toward his ball.

Then there was a blinding flash of blue light from the bunker and a cloud of smoke drifted across the green towards us.

"No!" said Okter. "Not again!" He sprinted across to the sand trap, me close at his heels. The two Secret Service guys followed behind. I noticed they didn't seem too worried that President Buckenberger had exploded. They were walking, not running. Obviously I wasn't the only one who knew this president wasn't human.

As we reached the top lip of the trap the smoke cleared, and we stared down at a pair of smoking golf shoes. That, and a twisted sand iron, were all that remained of the president.

I noticed the faint outline of something square that lay just under the sand. The blast must have blown enough sand out of the way for it to be revealed.

Okter shot a reptilian glance in my direction so I gave an impression of a dumb dog who hadn't seen a thing. To be honest, it wasn't much of a stretch. His gaze lingered a little longer than I was comfortable with, but I just chased my tail and, eventually, he looked away. They bundled the blackened shoes up in a box and we buzzed back to the White House in a big black car.

At the White House, Okter met up with Ms. Masters and they went into a huddle.

"It happened again," said Okter, lifting the scorched golf shoes from the box. "Looks like the micro-granulation flange gasket blew this time."

"I don't care what it is," hissed Masters, hitching her glasses. She flicked a sharp red nail at Okter. "Just get it straightened out! We don't have much time before the switch."

Okter seemed to consider arguing, and then thought better of it. The pair of them stalked off down the corridor, wisps of smoke trailing behind from the golf shoes. I let out a very long breath.

Vernon drifted up.

"How's it going?" he said. "Been having fun?"

I took a deep breath and told Vernon that the president had been replaced by a robot that had blown to bits on the dogleg sixth, whatever that was. When I got to the end, Vernon looked suitably impressed. Then he told me he had something to show me.

"This *is* all tied up with the disappearing dogs," he said. "I'm sure of that. But you don't need to worry about the president disappearing."

"Why not?" I said, a little snappishly.

"Because he's sitting in the Oval Office talking to a bunch of people and eating ham sandwiches," said Vernon. "Come and take a look."

And, leaving me openmouthed in the hallway, he padded off towards the West Wing.

After a coupla secs of goggling like a geek, I trotted after him.

What was going on?

CHAPTER 7

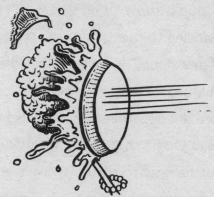

Screams, Queens, and Coconut Cream

Sure enough, when we snuck into the Oval Office, there was President Buckenberger sitting in the middle of a large group of well-dressed humans. We parked ourselves behind a sofa and had a conference.

"See?" said Vernon. "You must have made a mistake. There he is."

"It must be another Robo Prez!" I said. "Don't you see? They're using fake presidents to hide the fact that the real Prez has been kidnapped until they can sort out their evil plan!"

"I don't know," said Vernon. "He looks pretty convincing to me . . ."

"They all do," I snarled. "*Until they explode!*"

I barged past Vernon and set out at a fair clip across the deep-pile rug towards Fake President 2.

"Bad Dog!" shouted Vernon. "Wait!"

But he was too late. I wasn't going to sit back and watch the leader of the Free World get snatched and do zippo about it. I'm a dog of action. I shot towards Fake Prez 2 like a hairy rocket, Vernon racing just behind, trying to stop me.

An elderly woman with a funny accent and a pink hat, and holding a large slice of coconut cream pie in her gloved hand, stepped in my way and smiled at me. She had two little corgi dogs on a leash.

"Oh, what a simply adorable little doggy!" she said.

"Outta the way, sister!" I snapped, knocking her and the corgis backward over a little table, plunging her face-first into the coconut cream pie.

"Oh, Your Majesty!" said a voice behind me, rushing to pick the silly woman up. The two corgis started barking furiously and raced after me, dragging the woman along after them.

"I say, old boy!" yelled one. "That is simply *the* most unsporting thing I have seen in my life!"

"We're going to knock your ruddy block off, you, you . . . you *bounder*!" yelped the other.

But I wasn't listening. I was on a mission.

The fake Prez looked over at the commotion and caught my eye. I barreled towards him, knocking a guy with a leopard-skin hat straight into two Secret Service guys. They fell into a heap of people shouting insults in Japanese. An angry-looking dude, his chest dripping with gold braid and medals, tried to catch me, but I shot between his legs. He cracked his head against a frilly lamp and electric sparks flew across the room. Oops.

Fake Prez 2 was in my sights and I leaped onto a flowery-patterned armchair to give myself something to launch my attack from.

"I suppose you think that wig's gonna convince everyone?" I yelped at Fake Prez 2, as I trampolined off the armchair cushions and onto the robot's head. I tugged at his ridiculous wig with fury, bracing my back legs against his ears and pulling up with all my strength.

"Yaarrrrgggggghhhhhnnnnnnnnnnnnaaarrrggggh!" screamed Fake Prez 2, and took off like a headless chicken around the Oval Office. He was doing a pretty good imitation of someone in great pain.

They must have programmed that into the sucker's hard drive, I said to myself, and doubled my efforts to get the wig off. I just hoped I could do it before he exploded. I saw Dr. Okter over in one corner, looking at me curiously. Ms. Masters was talking to him and she too had an expression on her face that looked like trouble. Rover was doubled over with laughter.

"Bad Dog!" shouted Vernon from somewhere below. "No!"

By this time the Secret Service guys had disentangled themselves. They sprinted after us, crashing through furniture and stomping over some of the bigwigs lying all over the floor.

I gave a little smile of satisfaction as I noticed Dr. Okter taking a nasty fall over the back of a sofa and clocking Masters with his teacup on the way down.

Vernon had reached the Fake Prez and was steadily climbing his left leg. It was taking him a while because the Fake Prez was whizzing around faster than a washer set to spin and the two corgis were yip-yapping at his heels. They'd managed to ditch the old English lady somewhere over by the window.

We all crashed to the floor with a splintering crack of wood and upholstery. Realizing I was getting nowhere with the hairpiece, I released the Prez's wig and chomped down on his knee. He gave a surprisingly realistic screech of agony as my fangs went in. I remember thinking that there was an amazing amount of blood gushing out, considering it was a robot. The fabric of the Fake Prez's pants ripped as I got ready for a second chomp, and I noticed a dark brown mole shaped like a banana just above the shinbone. *S'funny*, I thought, *why would a robot have a mole?* And, just as soon as I'd had that thought, another popped into my head. If this was a fake president, why did he smell like a real one? But before I could work out the answer to those two little questions, a Secret Service dude grabbed me around the throat and gave me a gentle strangle, and everything went blaaaaaack . . .

80

Well.

It turned out that it wasn't a fake president after all. It was the real one. And the real President Buckenberger needed eighteen stitches in a nasty leg wound, plus corrective hair transplants after I had pulled out most of his hair.

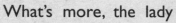

What's more, the lady who got a face full of coconut cream pie and was dragged around the Oval Office by a pair of hysterical corgis was none other than Her Majesty the Queen of Great Bognor or some such place. She was at the White House because her husband was taking part in the golf tournament. The other bigwigs had been knocked around, too, and none of them were very happy about it. Rover, of course, had laughed his socks off, the little freak.

And me? After doing all that, I figured that it was only a matter of time before I joined Blackie, Spotty, Toffee, Fudgee, and all those other very dead dogs out under the lawn. I had fouled things up big time. I lay back on my blanket in the White House kitchen where I'd been sent, and waited for dawn.

Dawn McGonagle, the White House cook, arrived about six o'clock and woke me up. Not that I'd had much sleep.

"You're wanted in the president's bedroom," she said. "Right away." A Secret Service suit stood in the doorway. This was it.

Chapter 8

My Reputation is on the Line

The Secret Service guy didn't say a word to me as he shooed me into the president's bedroom. He did speak into his little radio mike.

"Huckleberry Hound confirming package delivered. Out."

"Th-th-that's all, Folks!" I quipped, but he just looked at me blankly. "You know, Daffy Duck? Pepé Le Pew? Loony Tunes? Oh, forget it." I turned and faced the music.

President Buckenberger was propped up on the bed wearing silk pajamas and flipping through a golf magazine. His leg was bandaged heavily. So was his head.

Next to the bed stood Ms. Masters. Tall and ghostly, she regarded me coldly over the top of her black-rimmed glasses. She tapped a pen in a brittle fashion against her sharp white teeth.

I considered my options and bravely opted for a complete grovel. Tail between my legs, I slunk nearer to the bed and began the grovel of my life.

"I'd just like to apologize, oh Mighty Leader, for every-thing," I started to whimper, when the Prez cut me off in a strange singsong voice, the voice that people use when talking to small children and cute pets.

"How's my ickle soldier feeling?" said President Buckenberger. "Did that nasty catty-watty give you a bad scarey-warey?" He looked at me, a sickly expression of sympathy pasted on his face. Masters looked like she was going to be sick and pretended to read some papers she held in her hand.

"I . . . erm," I said, confused. "What are you saying?"

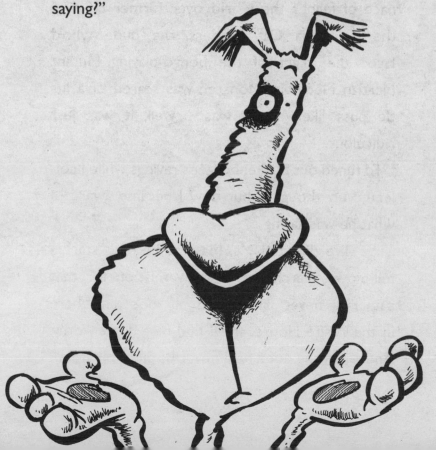

"You must have had quite a fright to run as fast as you did," said Buckenberger. "With that vile brute chasing you all over the Oval Office."

"*Vernon?*" I said, reeling. "You thought that *Vernon* was chasing *me?*" I was outraged. In fact, I was more than outraged; if this kind of thing ever got out, my street rep would take a heck of a beating. The idea that I, Bad Dog, menace of felines the world over, former chief of the California Cat Bashers, the dude who'd faced the might of the bongo-playing Mutant Martian Meowbag Monster, was scared of a little puss like Vernon was . . . well, it was just ridiculous.

I'd tuned out Buckenberger's ravings while I collected my thoughts, but now I became aware of what he was saying.

". . . I've directed Ms. Masters here to start a full-blown search and destroy mission for that cat. I've never liked cats. If he's anywhere in the White House, she'll find him, don't worry. And when she does, he'll never bother you again."

The Prez beamed at me and ruffled the top of my head.

Masters gave me a wintry little smile and nodded. "Oh yes, we'll take care of you," she said. "You can count on that."

This looked bad. Not just for my reputation, and not just for Vernon's skin. It was bad because, without Vernon, my chances of getting to the bottom of the disappearing dog mystery were sunk. And if I didn't find out what was going on, that meant that I was sunk, too. Sunk about six feet under the White House lawn with a nice hunk of marble to finish me off.

I *had* to find Vernon. And I had a pretty good idea where he might be.

I scooted out of the presidential bedroom and ran straight into Rover. He gave me a glare that should have come with a health warning.

"I don't know how you got out of that one, you *peasant*," he hissed. "But I want you to know that I'm on to you. And I know you're in cahoots with that creep Sangster."

I snarled at Rover and he flinched. "Don't tempt me," I snapped. "In the joint we ate dogs like you for breakfast. Now get out of my sight!" I jumped at him and Rover gave a squeal and zipped off down the corridor.

Meanwhile, I had a case to solve, and right now I needed my feline sidekick. I legged it down to the basement and followed my nose to where I knew Vernon would be holed up.

The boiler room.

Sure enough, he was there, wedged under a pile of old blankets in one corner. He was overjoyed to see me, and celebrated by picking up a shovel and smacking me over the head with it.

"Moron!" he shouted. "Dingbat! Dipstick! Idiot!" He punctuated each new insult with a clang of the shovel on my noggin.

I said nothing. After all, he was right. I deserved it.

After a minute or two, Vernon calmed down and we talked.

I filled him in on what the Prez had said.

"Oh, great, now I'm Public Enemy Number One."

"I don't think it'll last once Mrs. Prez hears about it. Besides, what about me?" I said. "Now everyone knows me as the dog who got chased by a cat. And not just any cat: a soft, fluffy, pampered, never-done-a-day's-work-in-his-life kind of cat who couldn't claw his way out of a wet paper bag. No offense."

"None taken," said Vernon. "But we need to get moving on this investigation. I've got an idea where we can start."

CHAPTER 9

KNEE DEEP IN STRANGE DISCOVERIES

Vernon led us through a series of little-used corridors and rooms. He knew every inch of that place and we slipped past the few people we did see without trouble. It seemed that the Prez's threat about Vernon hadn't got past Mrs. Prez.

"Where are we going?" I whispered.

"Just wait and see," said Vernon. "If my hunch is right this could be interesting."

We passed through a small hatch, and I realized that we had got into the ventilation system.

"Now, this is where you have to pretend to be a cat," said Vernon. "Try and make no noise whatsoever."

I did my best, tiptoeing along the metal duct. Every sound seemed to boom out, amplified by the pipes. Up ahead, I could see Vernon inching towards a hatchway. When I reached it, I saw that we were peering into the corridor directly outside a familiar-looking door. A marine was standing rigidly in front of it. It was the door I had seen Ms. Master and Dr. Okter slipping through when I'd arrived at the White House a couple of days ago. We pushed on along the shaft for a few yards and looked down through another hatchway. This time we could clearly see into the room; it was empty.

I loosened the hatch and we dropped to the floor. Vernon dropped down softly, landing on his paws. I cleverly used my head to cushion my fall.

It was an ordinary office. A plain wooden desk, blue office chair, wastebasket, filing cabinet, computer, portrait of President Buckenberger. This was it?

I looked at Vernon. He had no suggestions.

"There has to be something hidden in here," he said. "Otherwise, why would they guard it?"

It was a good point.

"Let's take a look around," I suggested.

There were odd blips and beeps coming from somewhere, and a faint chemical smell hung in the air. I followed the smell around the bare room. It seemed strongest close to the Prez's portrait. I lifted it to one side and looked underneath. There was a big red button on the wall.

"Go on," said Vernon. "Press it!"

"You press it!" I said. "For all we know that button could be the trigger for this whole place to self-destruct. It could be the final th —"

I stopped yammering, mainly because Vernon had leaped up and pressed the button.

The entire wall we had been standing next to slid up into the ceiling, and we stepped through into an enormous dark room.

It was a laboratory. In the gloom I could see large glass tanks filled with water and oddly shaped objects, softly burbling away. Computer LEDs and digital readouts supplied most of the light.

Around the edge of the room, stacked on shelves from floor to ceiling, were glass jars containing various dead animals: lizards, snakes, monkeys.

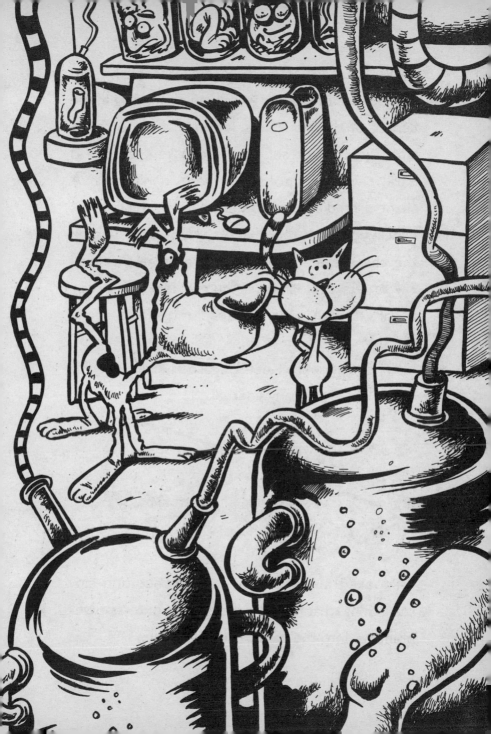

We glanced at each other nervously and approached one of the water tanks standing in the center of the lab. Wires fed into the top and a small green light set into the base cast jagged dark shadows into the gloom behind us. A shape drifted around inside, moved by the bubbles dancing through the fluid. As we pressed nearer, the shape came into focus. Vernon gave a small cry as we saw it was a human leg. There was a dark brown banana-shaped mole just above the shin.

"The President's Knee!" I gasped. "I'd recognize it anywhere!"

I looked a little closer at the knee and saw something that looked like a computer power point set into the banana-shaped mole.

In the other tanks, various bits of robot presidents bobbed around. One particularly revolting one contained nothing but presidential bottoms.

On the wall were detailed drawings and computer printouts of various parts of the president. A foot here, an elbow there. There was a half-constructed plastic model of the Prez's hand lying on a bench. Little wires and motors and computer chips were scattered everywhere.

On one bench were the scorched golf shoes I'd last seen in the bunker at Glistening Pines.

"Okter had those," I said. "He's definitely in on all this."

"Look at this," whispered Vernon. He was standing next to a table on which there was a shape covered with a blue sheet. It was a human shape . . . with one difference. It had no head.

"I wonder what happened to the head," said Vernon.

"I don't care if it's gone to Alaska," I said. "As long as I'm not around when it comes back."

By now I was ready to hit the road and give up on The Mystery of the Disappearing Dogs altogether. What with headless figures wafting around secret laboratories, jars full of knees, fresh graves, and exploding golfers, it was all getting a little too intense for this small pooch. I thought about aborting the mission.

"This place should be renamed the Fright House," I said. Vernon's reply surprised me.

"Fellow Americans, I come before you today not as a leader but as a friend."

I was about to ask Vernon what on earth he was yammering on about when I realized he hadn't said a word. We both looked over toward the darkened corner where the voice had come from.

"You first," I said, unselfishly pushing Vernon forward and casually picking up a length of metal pipe that was lying on a table.

"Me? Why me? You're the one who needs to find out what's going on," said Vernon, revealing himself to have the backbone of a plate of whipped cream.

He gave me a look, but started to move forward.

The voice got louder as we neared the corner. We couldn't see anyone.

"We have got to grasp the nettle, folks, there will be no increase in Texas, I'm going to take a five-iron off the tee cup and saucer please move right along inside, there will be no hiding place God Bless America, where's the fish? Cabbage, baggage, marriage . . ."

"It sounds like a total *psycho*! Where's it coming from?" said Vernon.

"It's coming from that fridge!" I hissed in a voice that would have been more at home in the mouth of a five-year-old girl. "Open it!"

"Are you completely mad?" said Vernon, glaring at me. "What do you mean 'open it'? Do I look like an idiot?" He flung his arm back to demonstrate how crazy he thought I was being, and banged the fridge door.

"Well, as a matter of fact —" I began, then stopped as the fridge creaked open, spilling light into the room. Sitting in there, talking complete nonsense and grinning like a maniac, was the head of President Buckenberger.

I don't mind admitting it: We screamed. Loudly.

When my heart rate got back down to a manageable level — oh, say 50,000 beats per minute — I realized that it was just a robot head doing the talking. Wires led down from its ears into a small power box sitting on the shelf next to it.

"Good evenong," said the head, winking an eye.

"Evenong. I mean, evening," I said, but the head didn't understand me any better than a real human. I closed the door gently and we backed away.

"I thought it might be you two," said the head.

"What does it mean?" I said. "How does that thing know about us?"

"It doesn't," said Vernon. "That wasn't the head talking."

We turned around.

Okter and Masters stood framed in the light from the door.

We were trapped.

CHAPTER 10

i Was Working in the Lab Late One Night

Okter and Masters wasted no time on being pleasant.

Despite putting up a titanic struggle, which mainly involved biting Okter in the butt, I was quickly strapped to one of the tables next to the headless Prez. Vernon had scratched Ms. Masters but it hadn't stopped him from getting the same treatment as me. He was swiftly locked down to the remaining table. We lay side by side, unable to move.

Masters spat some very rude language in the direction of Vernon and dabbed at her face with a handkerchief. The two of them shrugged into laboratory whites and started to flick switches and move equipment into place. Harsh strip lights flickered to life and the electronic hum of computers filled the laboratory.

"What are they doing?" whispered Vernon.

"I have no idea," I said. "But I know I don't like it." There were no two ways about it — the two of us were in deep, deep doggy-doo.

"Can it, you little pests!" shouted Masters in a steel-tinged voice. "Your yapping will get you nowhere."

The two of them wheeled a large metal pod into the center of the room and attached heavy-duty cables to ports mounted on the top. Okter wheeled in various bits of equipment and attached some of it to the pod. He grabbed a metal cap and rammed it on my head.

This didn't look promising. Masters stood and watched, a gleeful expression on her sharp features. Her eyes glinted like polished stones.

"This dog might be just the ingredient we've been looking for!" said Masters. "Those fools are going to regret choosing that baby-kissing buffoon over me! I should have been the next president, not that idiot Buckenberger! I was the best, the most qualified, the clearest thinker!"

"Too bad the voters didn't like you," muttered Okter under his breath, as Masters shot a nasty glare in his direction.

Okter flicked a switch and slipped a pair of industrial ear-protectors over his head. He joined Masters behind a protective wall. She, too, put on dark glasses and ear-protectors.

"Transmutation sequence activated," a metallic voice piped up. "Ten, nine, eight . . ."

The lights dimmed, and flashes of electricity jumped from one piece of odd-looking equipment to another. With a sound like a jet engine turning over, the pod began to vibrate — slowly at first, then faster and faster, until it started to blur. Blinding-white shafts of light shot from inside the pod and the noise in the lab built to almost unbearable levels.

My brain felt like it was being sucked from the top of my head and little rivers of electricity ran the length of my body. My fur stood on end and the pod seemed to soften at the edges like an out-of-focus photo. With one final boom, the pod stopped vibrating and the noise wound down to silence. Inside my noodle, my little brain flopped around like a landed fish.

"I think your smoothie's ready," I managed to gasp out to Masters, but the sarcasm was lost on her.

She stepped forward and released the bolts on one side of the pod. From inside came a low growl. A shape stepped from it into the light.

It was a dog.

This was no ordinary dog. It was massive, like a truck with legs. Beneath its dark fur, ropes of heavy muscle rippled and flexed. Its eyes glowed from the shadows below its brow. Perfect white teeth gleamed as it emerged into the lab. It flicked its eyes towards the two of us and I had a brief feeling that there was something familiar about this super-hound.

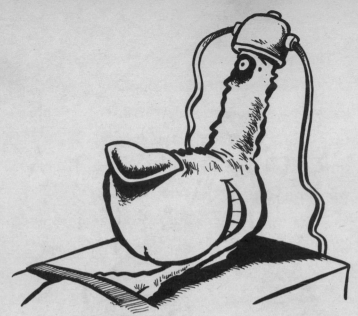

"Say," I said, as the dog drew itself up to its full height. "Have you been working out?"

"Careful, Bad Dog," said Vernon. "Let's not upset it."

"Upset it? This is a dog! One of us. Well, one of me, if you know what I mean. Maybe it'll help us."

"I wouldn't be so sure of that. Check out that smell."

"What smell?" I said.

Vernon looked at me pityingly. "Exactly. This thing doesn't smell of anything, least of all dog."

Then I got it.

We were looking at RoboDog. And as we looked at it more closely I realized with horror that we'd seen this pooch before. Except the last time we'd seen him, he'd been a stuck-up snob wandering around the White House.

"It's Rover!" I yelped. A souped-up, muscle-bound, robotic version of him, but it was still recognizably Rover. Vernon gasped. Rover had been transformed into a RoboDog!

"Magnificent!" trilled Masters. "I think we may finally have achieved one of our objectives, Doctor."

"Let me check," he said, pressing some buttons on a handheld gizmo. Instantly Rover sprang to attention.

As Okter's scaly hands twisted the controls, the dog responded. He rolled over, he played dead, he saluted. At one point his ears whirled around and he took off like a big hairy helicopter around the laboratory.

When he landed he snapped back to attention and, in a metallic voice, said, "Operative Rover 5000 reporting for duty, sir!"

Okter and Masters had built a remote-controlled RoboDog.

"That's enough of the party tricks," said Masters, looking over at us two. "Let's put him to work."

"Very well," said Okter. "And we need to straighten out a few of those little problems the PRX2 is having, too."

"I don't call exploding a 'little problem,' Doctor," said Masters icily. "But you are right, they do need straightening out. Just do it quickly. Time is running out."

Okter turned to Rover and casually waved his reptilian hand in our direction. I gave him my best cheesy grin.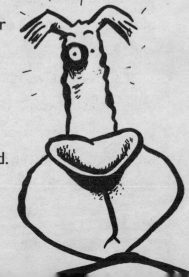

"Terminate them," he said.

I stopped smiling.

CHAPTER 11

A Likely Tail

Masters and Okter toddled off, probably to twiddle some dials and hatch some more fiendish plots in a corner of the lab. We were alone with Rover.

"This is a twelve-zillion-kilowatt, high-definition, military laser beam," he helpfully explained. "It can cut through forty layers of armor plating like a hot knife through butter." He adjusted the apparatus and spoke again.

"It will have no trouble making its way through you two." He chuckled metallically.

"If he's going to kill us, why doesn't he just stomp us?" whispered Vernon. "What's with all this *Star Wars* stuff?"

"Sssshhh!" I hissed back. "Don't give him any ideas. Maybe he just wants to scare us, you know, get information out of us."

I looked at the Rover 5000. "C'mon, man," I said. "You're a dog, I'm a dog. Let's work something out here. It doesn't have to be like this. Besides, I think you might have quite a few of my brain cells knocking about in your hard drive somewhere. And, believe me, I didn't have that many to spare. You owe me."

"And don't forget *me* while all this dog-bonding stuff is going on," piped up Vernon.

"It's too late for all that," said Rover. "I have my orders. Besides, I don't like you. You smell."

"Me?" I gasped. "I get *this* from a metallic mutant who's about to barbecue a couple of innocent fluffy little household pets? You're a disgrace to your breed, you freakin', lousy, stinkin', no-good, computer-chipped chihuahua!"

"I'd like to completely distance myself from those comments," said Vernon. "They don't represent my views at all."

We got no response. Rover was on a mission.

He pressed a switch and the laser hummed to life. A thin, red beam began tracking up the table toward me. I made a last effort at some pointless bravery.

"You don't expect us to talk, do you?" I sneered.

"No, I don't expect you to talk, Mr. Bad Dog," said Rover as he walked away, sounding like an old spy movie. "I expect you to die."

I looked at Vernon.

"Any bright ideas?" I said. The laser was only a few inches from my soft parts and, of all my parts, I was very, *very*, fond of my soft parts. "Any time. No hurry," I added.

"No need to get snarky," huffed Vernon. "We're in the same boat."

"Yeah, except my piece of the boat's got a freakin' laser cutting it in two!" I squeaked. "Get thinkin'!"

I frantically looked around for anything that might help us; an anti-laser device or a handy troop of cavalry, for example. Suddenly my eyes fell on Rover's remote control. Okter had left it on a tray next to my table. It was just out of reach. Typical.

"Use your tail!" said Vernon, who'd spotted the same thing. "Flick it over here!"

I squirmed a couple of smidges nearer to the remote control, bringing my butt even closer to the fast-approaching laser.

"I can't flick my tail!" I said to Vernon. "I can only wag it!"

"Then wag it!" said Vernon. "Quick!"

"I can't wag on command," I said. "I have to be happy about something. It's a dog thing."

"Good grief! Erm, I don't know, just think about bones or something!" said Vernon. I tried to visualize a big juicy bone, but it kept dissolving into nothing.

"No good," I said. "Think of something else! Quick!"

"What else do you like? Er, lampposts! Think about lampposts, hundreds of them, all smelly and waiting!" said Vernon.

"No good! This laser's almost singeing my waterworks! I can't concentrate on lampposts at a time like this!"

"Well, what *do* you most like doing?" said Vernon, exasperated.

And then it came to me. I had almost forgotten, what with Bentley Sweetlord's training, and with all this buddying up to Vernon. The thing I liked most of all, the thing that floated my boat every time was . . . *chasing cats*! And now the fear of being terminated had cut through all that Cataholics Anonymous stuff. I began to remember the sheer pleasure of running down a couple of those little suckers and the old tail started to flap like crazy.

"That's it!" shouted Vernon. "A little more!"

My tail caught the remote square on the side and it sailed neatly across onto Vernon's table. Now, a cat's tail is very different from a dog's. A cat can more or less do anything it likes with its tail. It could probably use it to perform open-heart surgery if the occasion arose. And now, Vernon, by craning his neck and delicately maneuvering his tail, began to operate Rover's remote control.

We could hear him coming before he got to us.

He galloped up and stopped next to my table, a confused expression on his face.

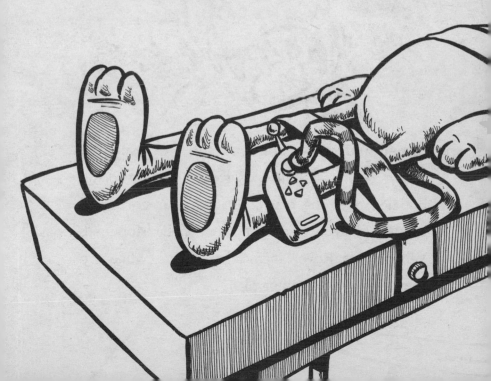

For a moment, I thought that Vernon had messed up the controls, as Rover opened his jaws and moved towards me.

Then, with a couple of chomps of his ginormous jaws, he cut me free! It was none too soon, either — my rear end had begun to smoke. Rover

turned and cut Vernon free and we gave each other a quiet high five. Masters and Okter, still huddled over the machines in the far corner of the lab, had not caught what had happened. Vernon put Rover into "idle" mode while we came up with a cunning plan.

CHAPTER 12

THE PLAN

"'Run'?" I said. "*That's* the cunning plan?"

"Well, do you have a better idea?" Vernon replied tartly.

As a matter of fact, I did. Perhaps that brain suction gizmo had worked in reverse because I suddenly felt like I was operating on overdrive.

"Pass the remote," I said. "And follow me."

Vernon raised one lazy cat eyebrow, but did as I asked.

"Now watch," I said to Vernon. I lifted the remote and Rover sprang into life. With a few twists of the paw I made him pick up the headless Prez from the table with the blue sheet and dump it in the pod.

"Right," I said to Vernon. "Hop up." I pointed at the empty table. "Under the sheet."

Vernon didn't hesitate. I followed him and we draped the sheet over us.

I could still see the lab by lifting a corner of the sheet.

"OK. Let's go fishin'," I said, picking up the remote.

Rover bounced over to where Okter and Masters were quietly bent over a table. I shuddered as I saw that Okter had a hold of Fake Prez's head. He held it casually, like he was about to toss it through a basketball hoop.

Behind them, Rover barked loudly and Masters nearly swallowed her tongue.

"Can't you put a volume control on that thing?" she snapped. "Sort it out."

I twiddled a few more controls and Rover rose into the air and pulled away from them. He crashed into a few jars and expensive-looking lab toys, making a whole lot of noise.

"Hey!" shouted Okter. "Come back!"

I maneuvered Rover back in our direction.

"What are you doing?" hissed Vernon. "You're leading them straight back to us!"

"Watch," I said. "They've taken the bait."

Rover passed us and I made him hover over the pod. Okter and Masters came scampering frantically after him, with Okter still holding the robot head.

Rover floated in midair above the pod like a big hairy balloon, as Masters and Okter passed our table, the blue sheet our only protection. With their backs to us, they looked up at Rover, who bobbed tantalizingly out of reach. He kept bumping into the animal containers stacked around the walls, and they rained down like glass bombs. The floor was slick with stinking chemicals and dead creatures.

"Come down, you overgrown Furby!" snapped Masters. "We haven't got time for this!"

"It won't respond," said Okter. "We need the remote."

This was it. Once they started looking for the remote, our chance was gone.

"Now!" I whispered to Vernon.

Vernon hopped onto my shoulders and we rose up from the table, the sheet still draped around us.

"Whooooooooo-ooooooooooo-oooooooo!" I wailed, doing my very best imitation of a really scary headless ghost in a neat Scooby-Doo cartoon. I know, it was a pretty desperate effort, but I was all out of good ideas and besides, it works for Scooby every freakin' week. It had to be worth a shot. And, what do you know, it worked.

Okter and Masters whirled around.

"Eeeeek!" squealed Okter. I'd never heard anyone actually say "Eeeeek!" before. I thought it was one of those things that people only said in comics. But Masters didn't bat an eyelid, and I thought we were finished.

"She's not going for it!" I whispered to Vernon, in between ghostly wails. He looked down.

"Just stick with it," he said. "Trust in Scooby. It's our only chance!"

Masters made a move toward us and I gave one last howl. The sheet fell off, but Okter still screamed and scrambled backward, away from us. He banged into the pod and, legs flailing on the slippery floor, he toppled into Masters, cracking her right on the noggin with the robot head.

She crashed to the floor like a felled tree.

Okter let go of the head as his legs wind-milled uselessly beneath him. It popped up into the air, stopped for a fraction of a second, and  caught my eye. "Hello Wyoming!" it said and dropped down into the pod. Then the lid slid shut and an electronic voice started a countdown. "Trans-mutation sequence activated. Ten . . . nine . . . eight . . ."

Okter looked at the pod and scratched his head.

There was a split second of silence and then the pod began to hum and vibrate, just as it had done earlier. Okter just stood and watched, still a little stunned from his fall.

Rover was still hovering in midair above the pod as it hummed away.

"What shall we do about him?" I said.

"Nothing," said Vernon. "I think it's time we got out of here. I don't really want to be around when that big microwave goes 'ding.'"

"Good point, well put," I said, and we hightailed it back towards the ventilation duct. Behind us the pod was winding down. There wasn't much time.

At the duct, we had to grab a desk and stack a couple of chairs on it to reach the ceiling. Vernon jumped into the duct and held out a paw to me.

I looked back down the darkened lab.

The pod ground to a halt and the lid slid open. White gas rose from inside. Okter stepped back from the edge.

"C'mon, man!" said Vernon. "Whatever's in there is definitely not good for your health!"

But I had to see.

As the gas cleared, a shape rose up from the pod, silhouetted in a blinding bright light.

I gasped.

"What is it?" said Vernon.

"It's — it's the president . . . and he's in one piece," I said, and scooted up into the duct. I hung my head back into the lab to haul the hatch shut behind us and took one last look. The mutant president looked up at Rover, still hovering on idle above the pod. The Prez pressed a finger to the side of his ear, rose up into the air, and slipped a leash around Rover's neck.

It was time to go.

Chapter 13

That Just About Covers It

Back in the boiler room we held an emergency meeting under a big pile of oily rags.

"What now?" I asked, not really expecting any sort of an answer. "I mean," I said, "let's just recap: So far we've come across spooky dog graves, golf-playing exploding fake presidents, secret laboratories, mutant robot dogs, brain-drain pods, a headless robot president, a knee factory, glass jars full of dead animals, a mad scientist (Okter), and his equally loony-toon boss (Masters), who want to replace the real president with a robot. Have I left anything out? Apart from the incident where I attacked the Queen of Somewhere or Other with a coconut cream pie and tried to pull President Buckenberger's hair out?"

"No," said Vernon. "That just about covers it." He continued, "The only question is: What are we going to do now? Masters and Okter aren't finished yet, not by a long shot. What is a long shot, anyway?"

"It's like a short shot, only longer," I snapped. "Sheesh! Just concentrate on the important stuff, will you, like keeping me alive."

"Talking of which, at least we know why they were using up dogs at that rate," said Vernon. "They were sucking stuff out of their brains to try and build the Rover 5000, then getting rid of them by staging 'accidents' around the White House."

"And if they needed to do that, pretend they were accidents, I mean," I said, excited, "it means that the real president doesn't know about Masters' little robot factory. We have to warn him!"

"The question is," said Vernon, "warn him about what? What are they up to?"

"It's not as if ole Buckenberger's gonna listen to us, anyway. He's too busy getting everything ready for that golf competition," said Vernon.

And then it came to me in a blinding flash: the complete picture, laid out nice and clear like I was looking down at one of those model train sets; all the bits and pieces in place, neat and tidy.

"Golf," I said.

"Golf?" said Vernon in a tone that suggested I should check my ears to see if any more of my nuts and bolts had broken loose.

"It's all about the golf tournament. That's when they're going to do it."

"Do what?" said Vernon.

"Replace the president," I said. "Don't you see? Masters is taking over. She couldn't get elected to be president herself. Remember that thing she said in the laboratory?"

"'Pass me that screwdriver, Okter'?" said Vernon, puzzled.

"No! She said: 'Those fools didn't pick me for the job!' There's only one thing she could have been talking about — being president! And if

she can't be president, she's going to be the next best thing: the hand that controls the puppet! They've been trying to perfect a remote-controlled president and they're close now, *real* close. I mean, the fake president I saw out at Glistening Pines was pretty good. They only have to iron out a few glitches, like stopping the knee from going ping, and the little matter of exploding under pressure, and they'll be ready to go. They've paved the way for this by already replacing all the *real* Secret Service guys. Remember those three Secret Service bods I saw sleeping?"

Vernon nodded.

"They weren't asleep, they were being *recharged* overnight, like big cell phones. The real ones have been sent to other duties one by one."

"But what about the dogs?" said Vernon. "Why do they want the *dogs?*"

"The finishing touch," I said. "Everyone knows that President Buckenberger loves dogs, right?"

Vernon nodded again.

"But dogs aren't so dumb as humans. Every dog they tried must have taken one sniff at the  fake president and realized what was going on. If they wanted a *robot* president, they needed a *robot* dog."

Vernon looked impressed. And rightly so. I was impressing myself. Maybe I should have half my brain sucked out by a fiendish mad scientist more often.

"So why are they rushing things now?" said Vernon.

"The golf tournament starts tomorrow," I said. "Some of the most important people in the world will be there. What better way to convince everyone that things are normal than by showing the world that the 'president' is happily playing golf? That's why Okter's been taking the robot presidents to Glistening Pines: to sort out any glitches. The headless robot in the lab and the head in the fridge must have been the one they were getting ready for tomorrow."

Vernon looked at me, a crestfallen expression on his face.

"But that means that . . ."

". . . that we finished the job for them," I said. "All they have to do is make the switch at Glistening Pines and we can kiss the White House goodbye!"

I paused for dra-matic effect and held up a paw.

"But there are a couple of things we've got up our sleeve, so to speak," I said, smiling. "The first is that we know exactly where the switch is going to be made."

"We do?"

"Remember me telling you about the big sand trap on the dogleg sixth? The place where the first fake Prez went up in smoke?"

Vernon nodded.

"Well, when the smoke had cleared, I noticed a square shape in the sand. Some of the sand must have been blown away by the blast." I looked at Vernon.

"A trapdoor!" he said, beating me to the punchline.

"And the other thing?" he asked.

I reached around and fished out a small black object.

"Rover's remote!" shouted Vernon.

"Where've you been keeping that?"

"Don't ask," I said, wincing. "It's something I learned in the joint."

I looked at my wrist. I don't know why, because I'd never worn a wristwatch in my life.

"What time is it?" I said to Vernon.

"How should I know?" said Vernon. "I'm a cat. All I know is that it's after breakfast and before dinner. I'm hungry, so I guess it's about five o'clock."

I smiled and jumped up.

"Let's go! We've got seventeen hours to save the president!"

I love getting to say stuff like that.

CHAPTER 14

MY LAST NIGHT AT THE WHITE HOUSE

Vernon came up with a top-notch idea about where we could lay low overnight.

"The presidential bedroom," he said. "It's the last place they'll look! And if they do find us there, you can rely on the real Buckenberger to help — don't forget he's a dog nut. We'll stow ourselves in there and hitch a ride over to Glistening Pines in the morning."

"We still haven't planned what we're going to do when we get there," I said.

"We'll figure something out," said Vernon.

The Prez's bedroom was miles away, over in the West Wing. We decided it'd be safer outdoors, so we headed that way.

Vernon eased the boiler room hatch up and we slipped out into the dark. We hadn't gone more than ten feet when a powerful beam of light carved through the night toward us.

"Quick!" I hissed, and bundled us both into a nearby bush. The beam swept over us but didn't stop. Clipped voices came from up ahead.

"Pepé Le Pew to Foghorn Leghorn. Sector Five confirmed clear. No sign of them. Over."

"Confirm position, Huckleberry Hound. Over."

"Look," said Vernon, pointing through the leaves. We looked and saw more flashlights sweeping the grounds. Silhouetted against the sodium lights from the city were three hulking figures. It was the robot Secret Service guys. They were looking for someone, and I didn't have to be a brain

surgeon to figure out it was us two who were being chased.

"I guess Masters woke up," said Vernon.

"And they know that we're the only ones who know what's going on. Get rid of us and the next time we see the Prez he'll have metal joints," I added. "C'mon, let's get moving."

We skirted along the flower beds, using our natural talents to help avoid the robots. Vernon could see clearly in the dark, and I could sniff out a spider's body odor at fifty paces. The trouble was, these robots didn't have much of a smell.

As we rounded the corner nearest to the president's bedroom, we saw the light was still on. As we had thought, Masters and Okter hadn't predicted that we'd make for Buckenberger's bedroom, and the search was concentrated over by the boiler room. We could see the beams cutting holes in the night sky behind us.

"I think we've made it," said Vernon. "All we've got to do is figure out a way to get up there."

He pointed at the balcony that fronted the Prez's room.

I was about to wrap my problem-solving skills around that when a hulking great black shape loomed

up ahead of us, and my street cred took another bashing as I jumped into Vernon's arms. Or I would have if Vernon hadn't fainted.

The shape moved into a patch of light from a nearby window.

It was Rover.

I guessed that the fake president had sent him out to look for us.

And here he was.

There was a moan from the floor as Vernon came to. As he looked up, Rover growled and moved toward us. I was about to say my prayers when I remembered something, and a broad smile crept across my mush.

"Get ready to say bye-bye," said Rover, laughing a little overdramatically, I thought.

Vernon looked paralyzed with terror but his mouth dropped open when I stepped forward fearlessly and held up a paw to Rover.

"Not so fast, you chunk of hairy metal," I said and whipped out the remote control. "Aren't you forgetting something?"

Rover's face fell. "Oh, no," he said.

"Oh, yes," I said and twisted the dial. Instantly Rover fell silent and his eyes glazed over.

"C'mon," I said to Vernon. "Hop on." I gave the remote another twiddle and Rover dropped to all

fours. We clambered up onto his back and his ears began to rotate. With a soft whirr, we rose into the air and floated gently up to the balcony. I guided Rover in for a perfect landing.

"I gotta get me one of these," said Vernon.

I parked Rover quietly in a corner and we trotted into the bedroom. We were taking a chance: I still didn't know how Mrs. President would react, but when we got inside she wasn't there. The president was practicing his putting again. Man, that guy likes to play golf.

When he saw us he dropped to his knees and ruffled the top of my head and started doing all that stuff that dog lovers do when they see a dog.

You know what I mean, rolling around on the carpet, play-wrestling, and, worst of all, baby talk.

Vernon smirked at me but at least I knew we were dealing with the real thing here.

In any case, Vernon didn't have time to enjoy poking fun at me. The door opened and Mrs. President swept in in a cloud of perfume and hair clips.

She laid eyes on Vernon and screamed, "Daaaaaarling! Come to Mummy!" She clutched him to her chest and Vernon almost disappeared from view. "Has the naughty doggy-woggy been hurting oo, possum?"

Vernon didn't reply to this (probably trying to avoid being sick) and eventually the first lady put him down. The president coughed and said the words I wanted to hear.

"I guess these two should stay here tonight."

CHAPTER 15

THE BIG FINISH

I stood alongside the first tee at Glistening Pines and looked out at the sparkling fairway unrolling in front of me like a great green velvet carpet. The sun shone, the birds tweeted, and everything was right with the world.

Apart from the fact that the President of the United States was about to be replaced by a robot controlled by an evil stick insect look-alike, that is.

The president, of course, was blissfully unaware of all this as he stepped onto the tee.

"On the tee: the President of the United States!" announced the announcer guy, beaming from ear to ear. Across the tee, Masters and Okter glared at us with barely disguised hatred.

The president shaped up to hit the ball when a strange grinding noise started to put him off. He whipped around and glared at where the sound had come from.

"Ms. Masters," said the president. "Could you stop grinding your teeth for a moment?"

The Prez drew back his club and with a clack of club on ball, the 12th Annual White House International Golf Challenge was under way.

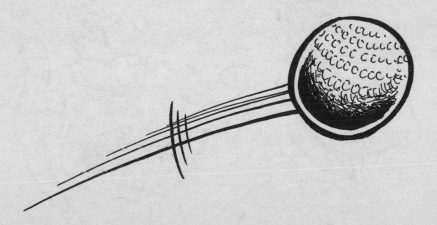

Vernon and I had woken in the presidential bedroom and stuck to the Buckenbergers like a bad rash. When the time came we'd hitched a ride in the presidential motorcade to the course. Masters had caught a glimpse of us and her look almost melted the limo door as we stepped inside.

On the way over, we'd done our best to explain what was going to happen: about the robots, the lab, the booby-trapped sand traps, the evil Ms. Masters, and reptile-boy Okter. But it all came out as a bunch of barking and mewing, and we could see that the Buckenbergers were not getting the picture. "Really," said Mrs. Prez, "what is *wrong* with these two?"

"We'll have to do this ourselves," said Vernon.

"Do what?" I said.

"Whatever we need to do."

Which brings us up to speed.

And speaking of speed, we were quickly running out of time. If the Prez knocked his ball into a sand trap he would be replaced faster than a faulty light bulb in a mineshaft.

President Buckenberger's golf tournament was a Pro-Am event. That is to say that as well as golf duffers like the Prez, there were real golfers playing alongside them. The Prez's golf partner was some guy with a weird name: Panther or Leopard or something. I know it was a cat name, anyway. And he was very good.

I looked around to check on Masters, Lizard Boy, and the rest of the robot brigade, but they were nowhere to be seen. Which worried me.

We reached hole four without a problem. There had been a hairy moment on the last hole, when the Prez had scuffed his third shot towards a nasty-looking sand trap. Fortunately, at the last moment, the ball clonked an elderly spectator on the forehead and rebounded safely onto the green. Everyone clapped. Apart from the old geezer who was knocked out cold.

The fourth was a short one. Leopard took his shot and pinged it straight onto the green, about four feet from the flag. He stepped away from the tee.

The Prez took a club from the bag and hunched over the ball. He drew the club back and snapped through nicely in what looked to be his best shot. The ball rose gracefully in a perfect arc against the blue sky . . . and sailed straight into a gigantic sand trap next to the green.

This was it, I knew. Masters and Okter must have been getting ready ahead of us on each hole. We rattled along in the golf cart toward the sand.

"What are we going to do?" said Vernon.

My brain was letting me down on the idea-producing front. I could think of nothing.

The president stepped from the cart. It had stopped moving, by the way. He selected his sand iron and walked towards the sand trap. Like the one on the sixth, this one was sheltered from view by a bank of trees. There was no choice — it was time for drastic action.

"Wish me luck!" I said to Vernon, and jumped down from the golf cart. I raced ahead of the Prez and into the sand. Out of the corner of my eye I noticed Masters and Okter back on the scene.

They were watching, horrified.

"What the . . . ?" spluttered the president as I seized the golf ball. If there was no ball then he couldn't play the shot, right? I'd got the ball between my teeth and moved off. Except that the ball was stuck. It didn't move. Okter and Masters had scrambled into action and the robot Secret Service guys were headed our way.

"Get him, you morons!" screamed Masters.

I turned back to the ball and gave a big tug. It moved, finally! Underneath the ball was a cable snaking through the sand.

"Stop!" shouted the president. "What do you think you are doing?"

As I pulled the ball, the sand shifted behind me and a trapdoor slid open. Like a maniac jack-in-the-box, the robot president popped up into view. He was dressed identically to the real Prez. There were screams from the crowd. Another trapdoor opened just behind the real Prez and I pulled him back in the nick of time.

"Whoa!" said Leopard, looking at the new fake Prez and taking a couple of steps back away from the lip of the sand trap.

The real Prez just goggled and made a face like a fish.

"It's too early!" wailed Okter behind me.

"Shut up, you idiot!" snapped Masters.

The real President Buckenberger shot a sharp look of understanding at Masters and Okter. The robot president just looked confused. But not for long. Masters fiddled with a device on her wrist and robot Prez moved towards the real Prez. The expression on his face had changed.

"You must die, you must die," he droned. Real President Buckenberger looked around at his Secret Service guys but they just stood watching. The real Prez turned back to the robot.

"I guess it's just me and you, you battery-operated freak," said the Prez, and hurled himself onto the robot. In a tangle of arms and legs and sand, they thrashed around trading blows and rolled out onto the green. I heard the clangs as President Buckenberger's fist connected with the robot's metallic frame, but in all the confusion I soon lost track of who was who. I wasn't the only one, from the looks on the faces in the crowd. One thing I

did know: For all his bravery the real Prez couldn't last long in a fight against a robot. And sure enough, one of the presidents was fading. President Buckenberger sank to the floor, the robot's hands around his neck.

"Stop him!" screamed someone in the crowd. There was a sudden surge of bodies and the robot's hands were prised from around the president's neck. He gasped and coughed for air.

With five or six people holding him, the robot couldn't go anywhere.

"Let me go, you idiots!" shouted the robot. "I'm the real president! I order you to release me!"

"Looks like it turned out okay," said Vernon.

I was about to agree with him when I noticed something odd about Masters. She was smiling.

"It's the old switcheroonie!" I said to Vernon. "They've got the wrong president!"

"What?" said Vernon. "But we all saw the robot strangling the president!"

"No! Masters programmed the robot to pretend to be losing the fight! She's fooled them!"

"How can we prove it?" said Vernon.

"The knee!" I said. "Remember the knee!"

"What?" said Vernon again, but I was already moving towards the robot president on the ground. Masters was fussing over him/it. Okter stood alongside.

I arrived and stood over the robot, who was doing a very convincing impression of a man who'd been attacked by a killer robot.

"I bet you think you're going to get away with it," I sneered. "Well, cop this!"

I lifted my hind leg and tinkled all over his knee. I'd remembered that the knees in the laboratory had all had computer power ports hidden in a mole. A little doggy water would short-circuit the robot and fry his wires in front of everyone.

"Take that!" I barked and waited for the electrical freak-out.

The robot president looked as if he couldn't believe what I'd done.

"But, but," he spluttered, "I love dogs!"

Masters laughed.

I began to have doubts about whether I'd peed over the right president.

"You dumb mutt," whispered Masters into my ear. "Do you think a little water's going to do anything to the PRX2?"

Masters and her oily sidekick both smiled, and I knew we had lost.

Just then, Vernon appeared at my shoulder. "Well," he said. "Did it work?"

I began to explain that it hadn't when I noticed a change coming over the robot president. On catching sight of Vernon, his upper lip curled back, and he began growling. A strange glow appeared in his eyes and he flipped over onto all fours.

He put his head low to the ground and I could see him tense as he locked eyes on Vernon.

"Okter," said Masters. "What's it doing? Stop it! He'll give the game away!"

"I can't!" said Okter frantically working his wrist remote. "It's not responding!"

"Er, Bad Dog," said Vernon. "If I didn't know better, I'd swear this robot thinks he's a . . ."

"A dog!" I finished for him, smiling the sweet smile of victory.

The robot president sat back on his haunches and howled like a wolf. Vernon made a break for it across the green and the robot president raced after him on all fours barking like a Rottweiler with its butt on fire.

By now I was rolling on the ground laughing my rear off. The people holding the real president released him and we all watched as the PRX2 chased Vernon back down the fairway.

Chapter 16

The End Part

"So, what happened?" said the Reverend Bentley Sweetlord the Fourth. "Why did the robot dude suddenly decide to chase the cat?"

We were in the exercise yard back at the City Pound. I'd been shipped back right after the shenanigans at Glistening Pines. You might have expected a little gratitude for all my efforts, no? You'd have been wrong. Vernon got all the glory while I was remembered as the dog who peed all over the President of the United States. The fact that he turned out to be a psycho robot seemed to be beside the point. All the TV cameras kept showing was me cocking my leg over what looked exactly like the president lying helplessly on the ground. The real Prez tried to let me stay, but his advisers were having none of it.

"It just doesn't sit right with the voters, Mr. President," said the new White House Chief of Staff.

Masters and Okter had gone, too. I'd heard that they were last seen wearing orange overalls and making licence plates down in some flyblown jail in Arkansas. Good.

Vernon, on the other hand, was greeted as if he'd cracked the mystery all on his lonesome. It probably helped that Mrs. Buckenberger was such a cat lover.

I turned back to Bentley. "What happened?" I said. "It was all down to what happened back in the lab. Remember I'd told you about getting my brain drained just before we escaped?"

Bentley nodded and I continued. "Well, some of it must have somehow gotten into the pod along with the rest of the robot president. When the pod did its stuff, the dude that came out was part robot . . . and part dog. Part Bad Dog to be exact."

I looked at Bentley. "And the part that was in the robot hadn't attended Cataholics Anonymous. When robot Prez caught a glimpse of Vernon, a million years of dog evolution kicked in and he just *had* to chase that cat. He never caught Vernon, though. He fell into an ornamental lake and all his wiring short-circuited. Masters had been wrong about that computer port on his knee: It was leaky. I'd just peed on the wrong leg."

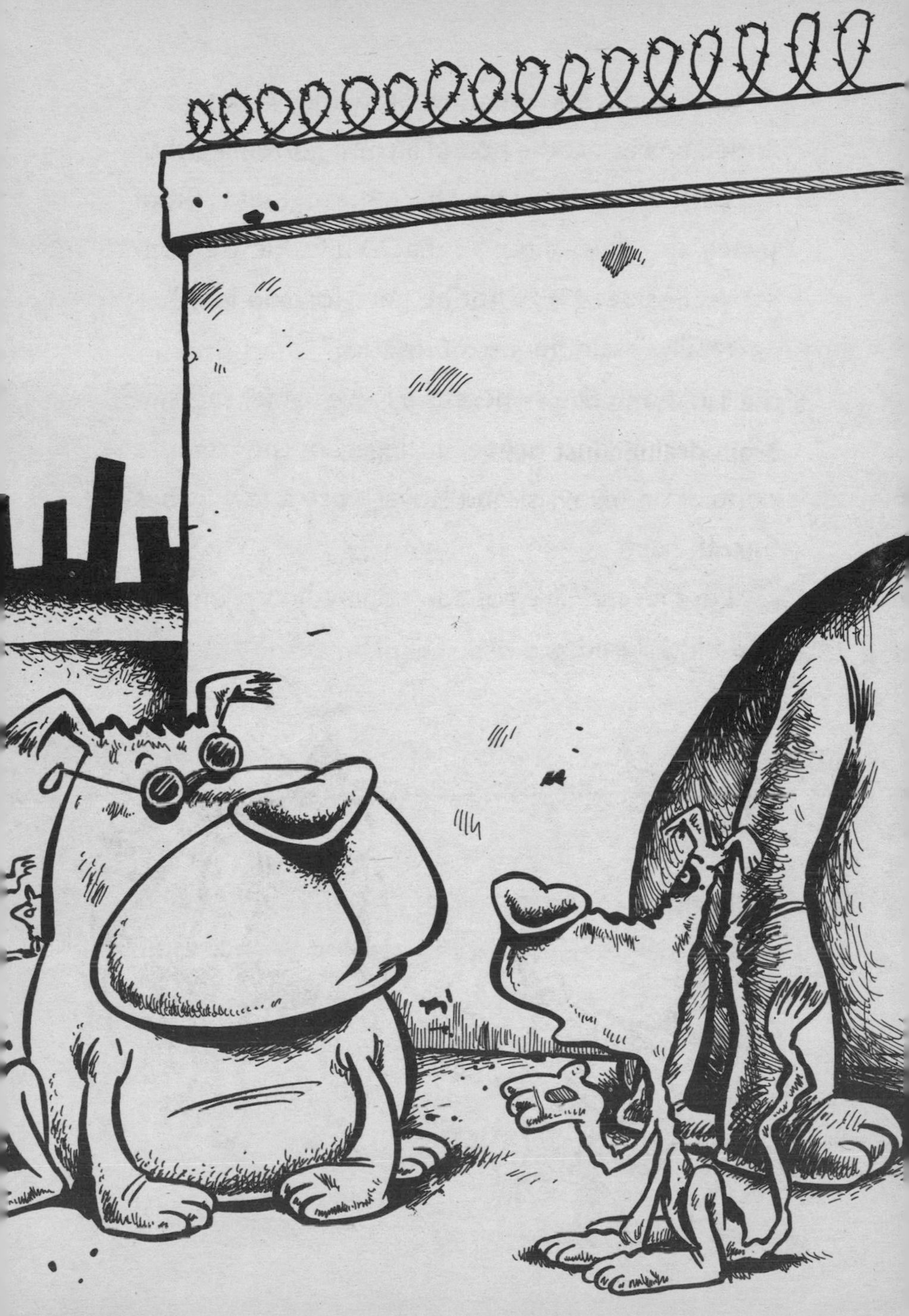

"Too bad," said Bentley. "You might not have ended up back at the pound if you'd gotten it right."

"Oh, I don't mind being back here," I said. "Bit of peace and quiet after all that White House nonsense. Besides, I may not be here for too long."

"Really?" said Bentley. "How so?"

I looked over to where the Rover 5000 sat happily staring into space. I fingered the remote control on my wrist and Rover rose a few inches into the air.

"Let's just say I've got someone who's promised me a lift," I said.